Disney
Beauty and the Beast

Read-Along
STORYBOOK AND CD

This is the story of *Beauty and the Beast*.
You can read along with me in your book.
You will know it is time to turn the page
when you hear the chimes ring like this. . . .
Let's begin now.

For information address Disney Press, 1101 Flower Street, Glendale, California 91201.

Printed in the United States of America

First Paperback Edition, January 2017 10 9 8 7 6 5 4 3

Library of Congress Control Number: 2015955209

ISBN 978-1-4847-7606-3

FAC-008598-17111

For more Disney Press fun, visit www.disneybooks.com

DISNEP PRESS

Los Angeles • New York

SUSTAINABLE FORESTRY INITIATIVE

Certified Chain of Custody
At Least 20% Certified Forest Content
www.sfiprogram.org
SFI-00993

Logo Applies to Text Stock Only

Once upon a time, a young prince lived in a giant castle. One cold night, an old beggar arrived and offered him a rose in return for shelter. He sneered at her gift and turned her away.

Suddenly, she transformed into a beautiful enchantress. Then she turned the Prince into a hideous beast!

The Enchantress also changed the castle servants into enchanted objects. Then she left behind a magic mirror and the rose. For the spell to be broken, the Prince would have to fall in love, and earn that person's love in return, before the last petal fell.

In a small village nearby lived a beautiful young woman named Belle. As she entered the town bookstore, the owner gave her a book as a gift.

"It's my favorite! Far-off places, daring sword fights, magic spells, a prince in disguise . . . Oh, thank you very much!" Belle rushed outside, reading as she walked.

Soon a hunter named Gaston walked up to her. He grabbed the book from her hands. "It's about time you got your nose out of those books and paid attention to more important things—like me."

Then Gaston's friend LeFou approached. He began to insult Belle's father, Maurice, who was an inventor.

"My father's not crazy! He's a genius!" Then Belle ran toward her father's cottage.

When Belle got home, she told her father that the townspeople were making fun of him.

"Don't worry, Belle. My invention's going to change everything for us." Maurice was hoping to sell his latest creation at the town fair. He hopped on his horse, Phillipe, and headed into town.

But Maurice got lost, and he and Phillipe ended up
in a dark, misty forest. All of a sudden, a pack of wolves
surrounded them! Phillipe reared and ran away.

Terrified, Maurice raced through the forest, with the wolves
right behind him. When he reached a tall gate, he opened it and
dashed inside. Then he slammed it shut on the angry wolves.

Belle's father looked up and saw a huge castle. He walked up to the front door and knocked.

"Hello? I've lost my horse, and I need a place to stay for the night."

"Of course, monsieur! You are welcome here!"

Maurice looked down to see a clock and a candelabrum staring up at him. "This is impossible! Why . . . you're alive!"

The candelabrum, named Lumiere, led him inside.

All of a sudden, a loud voice boomed. "There's a stranger here!" In the shadows lurked a large, hulking figure. It was the Beast!

Maurice pleaded with him. "Please . . . I needed a place to stay."

But the Beast ignored him and dragged him away.

At home, Belle heard a knock on the door.

"Gaston!"

"Belle, there's not a girl in town who wouldn't love to be in your shoes. Do you know why? Because I want to marry you!"

Belle turned his proposal down. She did not like the conceited bully. Disappointed, Gaston left.

A little while later, Belle went outside and found Phillipe all alone. "Phillipe! What are you doing here? Where's Papa?"

The horse whinnied anxiously. Frightened, Belle quickly leaped onto Phillipe, who led her to the mysterious forest. Soon they spotted a castle in the distance.

Belle ran toward the castle and snuck inside. She wandered down a dark, deserted hallway. A few moments later, she found her father locked in a tower. "Papa! We have to get you out of there!"

Suddenly, she heard a loud voice call out from the dark shadows. "What are you doing here?"

Belle gasped. Standing in front of her was a giant beast! "Please, let my father go. Take me instead!"

"You would . . . take his place?"

When Belle promised to stay with the Beast forever, he released Maurice.

Back in the village, Maurice ran into a tavern. There he spotted Gaston and his friends.

"Please, I need your help! A horrible beast has Belle locked in a dungeon!"

The crowd laughed, convinced that he was crazy. But Maurice's wild story gave Gaston an idea. . . .

Inside the castle, the Beast showed Belle to her room. "You can go anywhere you like, except the West Wing."

"What's in the West Wing?"

"It's forbidden!" The Beast stomped off.

Belle ran into her bedroom. "I'll never escape from this prison—*or* see my father again!"

Her new friends—the enchanted household objects—tried to cheer her up, but Belle was too upset.

Later that night, Belle was feeling a little better. Lumiere led her into the dining room. The napkins, dishes, and spoons danced as the serving pieces carried in tasty food. Belle was delighted!

After dinner, Belle wandered into the forbidden West Wing. There she found the enchanted rose, shimmering beneath a glass dome. She reached out to lift the cover.

But the Beast had been secretly watching her! He was very angry. "I warned you never to come here! Get out!"

Terrified, Belle fled the castle.

Outside, Belle
found Phillipe. They
galloped toward
the village. All of
a sudden, a pack of
hungry wolves circled
them! They crept
toward Belle, baring
their large white fangs.

Just then, the Beast appeared! The wolves began to attack him. With a loud roar, the Beast fought off the wolves. As they ran away, the Beast collapsed in pain. Belle knew this was her chance to escape, but she could not leave him.

"Here, lean against Phillipe. I'll help you back to the castle."

When they returned, Belle tended to the Beast's wounds and thanked him for saving her life.

The Beast smiled. To show how grateful he was, he gave her access to the beautiful castle library.

Meanwhile, Gaston was plotting to put Belle's father in an insane asylum. The only way he wouldn't do it was if Belle agreed to marry him. Gaston was convinced that soon she would become his wife.

As more time passed, Belle and the Beast became good friends. One day, she watched as he tried to feed some tiny birds. She realized that he was kind and gentle, despite his gruff appearance.

One night, Belle and the Beast dressed up for a fancy dinner. The Beast even remembered his table manners. They both had a wonderful time.

After dinner, Belle taught the Beast how to dance. They glided gracefully across the floor. The Beast had never been happier.

He asked Belle if she, too, was happy.

"Yes, I only wish I could see my father. I miss him so much."

"There is a way."

Moments later, the Beast brought Belle the magic mirror.
When she wished to see her father, Maurice appeared in the glass.
He was lost in the woods.

The Beast saw the unhappy look on Belle's face. He decided to
let her go—even if it meant he would never be human again. He
handed Belle the mirror. "Take it with you, so you'll always have a
way to look back and remember me."

Soon Belle found her father. But moments later, a group of men grabbed Maurice to take him away!

Gaston put his arm around Belle. "I can clear up this little misunderstanding—*if* you marry me."

"I'll never marry you. My father's not crazy! I can prove it!" She showed Gaston the magic mirror. An image of the Beast appeared in it.

Gaston shouted, "I say we kill the Beast!" Then he and the villagers headed toward the castle.

When the townsfolk arrived, Gaston forced the Beast onto the roof. As they fought, Gaston lost his balance and fell to the ground.

The Beast suddenly collapsed. Belle ran toward him. She cried, "No! Please! I love you!"

Seconds later, the Beast sprung into the air. He was
surrounded by a shimmering glow. Belle had told the Beast
that she loved him, which meant that the evil spell that had
been cast on him—and all of the household staff—was broken!

The Beast transformed back into a handsome prince!

"Belle, it's me!"

"It *is* you!"

True love had broken the spell, and Belle and the Beast lived happily ever after.